The Rainbow Ribbon

Candace Nadine Breen

To all those who dare to dream.

To the loves of my life:

Peter, Aiyanna, JR, Vono and Alfredo.

Long ago and far, far away was a little village of worker ants who lived on an ant farm. They worked day and night, night and day, every single day of the week. It was tough work being a worker ant but no one complained. All the ants knew was work and they loved to work... all except one ant. His name was Herbin and he spent his days gazing up into the sky while lounging beneath an old oak tree. He was a dreamer ant and he loved to think about things that no other ant understood, like colorful unicorns, magical fairies, puffy clouds and sparkling rainbows. He had nine thousand nine hundred ninety-nine brothers and sisters who also lived on the ant farm and who, like all the other ants, worked every day and every night. Herbin just liked to dream.

One day, Herbin's parents approached him. His father said, "Why do you always look into the sky? There's nothing up there. You have nine thousand nine hundred ninety-nine brothers and sisters who are worker ants! We are all descendants from worker ants! You are a worker ant and worker ants work! Work is real and you need to work!"

"Rainbows are real, too." Herbin said.

"Blah! If you can't touch it, it isn't real. Work is real!"

"Herbin is a dreamer, dear." Herbin's mother chimed in.

"He is a lazy ant! Worker ants work!" Herbin's father angrily said and stormed away, back into the worker fields. Herbin began to cry.

"Oh, honey, your father just wants what's best for you. He loves you so—"

"He doesn't understand me! I am NOT a worker ant!" Herbin was so upset that he decided that he would run away… away from his nine thousand hundred ninety-nine brothers and sisters, away from the ant farm in the little village, away from his mom and dad. He ran and ran and ran and ran as fast as his little legs could carry him. He was running away, forever.

Sad, hungry, and tired, Herbin happened upon a little cottage. He noticed that the cottage was a little crooked-looking, and a little ugly-looking, and was the color of wet dirt. Even though Herbin was a little frightened, he was hungry and wanted to rest so much that he was brave enough to knock on the door.

"Go away!" shouted an angry voice from inside.

"Please, I am just a little ant and want to rest and, perhaps, you could share some of your food?" Herbin begged. The door suddenly swung open and out stepped a very dirty and very grumpy old gnome.

"I don't have any food to share!" shouted the gnome, crossing his arms, angrily.

"A bed? Perhaps you could share a resting place in your cozy cottage?" Herbin pleaded, again.

"No, I don't have that to share, either!" the grumpy gnome shouted before slamming the door. Herbin had no choice but to continue his journey. Herbin walked and walked and walked until he reached a stone path. At the end of the path was a cozy little hut. There was smoke coming from the chimney and the door of the hut was open.

Herbin slowly crept up to the door. He heard humming and could smell the sweet aroma of honey biscuits drifting through the door. Herbin's mouth began to water as his belly grumbled with hunger.

"Come in, Herbin my friend." a voice from inside the cabin said. Herbin was suddenly afraid. Who could know his name when he was miles and miles away from the ant farm in the village where he lived with his mother, father and his nine thousand nine hundred ninety-nine brothers and sisters? Surely, no one else would know him.

"Don't be afraid, Herbin. Please, come in." the voice said again. Mustering up all the courage in his little ant body, Herbin slowly entered the tiny hut. Inside he saw an old man wearing a wizard's hat and a wizard's robe. The old man was also holding a wizard's wand.

"My name is Winton." The wizard said. "I knew you would come here soon. Sit and share some biscuits and apple cider with me." Herbin couldn't contain himself. He ran to the table and gobbled up as many sweet biscuits as he could and he even drank a whole glass of apple cider.

"You are descended from a long line of worker ants and yet you choose to be a dreamer ant." the wizard said when Herbin had finished eating.

"I just wish Mom and Dad would stop bothering me about being a worker ant. What is wrong with dreaming?" Herbin said angrily.

"Ah, I don't mean to insult you, dear friend. I want to help you."

"How could you help me? I don't want to be like everyone else. I want to think about beautiful things."

"And I can help you help your mom, your dad and your nine thousand nine hundred ninety-nine brothers and sisters to think about beautiful things, too."

"How could you do that?"

"What if I told you that you could catch a rainbow and take it to your village for everyone to see? "

"That would be great, if that were true. My father doesn't believe in rainbows." Herbin said as he looked down sadly.

"Ah, but rainbows are very real, dreamer ant. If you trust me, I can tell you where to go to get a golden ribbon – a special magical golden ribbon - that will help you lasso the rainbow, drag it down from the sky, and take it to your village for everyone to see!"

"But I am such a small ant. I cannot do such a big thing."

"But you can. Even though you are but a small ant, it only takes a big belief in yourself. I will tell you how to do this, if you want to give it a try, but you have to promise me that you won't give up no matter what happens. Do you want to give this a try?" asked the wizard.

"Yes, I want to try."

"And you promise not to give up?"

"Yes, I promise."

"Great!" Winton the wizard leaned in close to Herbin as the two of them sat at the small wooden dinner table. "Then, you cannot tell this to anyone, because the golden rainbow ribbon is only meant to be handled by the one who believes in the world of dreams. You must first find the pond where the frog family lives. It is about a half day's journey from here. The frogs are my friends and, if you give them this special bag of flies, they will tell you where to go." Winton handed Herbin a clear bag of live flies that had been sealed at the top.

"Do not lose the bag and don't stop until you reach the frog family. They won't believe that you have been sent by me until you produce this magic bag of flies. It is important that you give this bag to them before you ask for their help."

"How will they tell me where to go next if I can't speak to them?" asked Herbin.

"Stand at the foot of the pond and stick one leg into the water. This will wake up Grandfather Frog who will ask you who you are and what you want. Tell him your name, tell him you were sent by me, and then tell him that you have brought a gift. The frog family loves my special flies. He will then tell you what you need to do next."

"I think I should go now before it gets dark."

"Why, yes! You are a smart little ant! Take this bag and some extra food for the journey." the wizard said, handing Herbin a sack of sweet biscuits that seemed to appear from nowhere.

"Now, get going and don't stop until you get to the pond!" Herbin thanked the wizard, bid him farewell, and set about his journey.

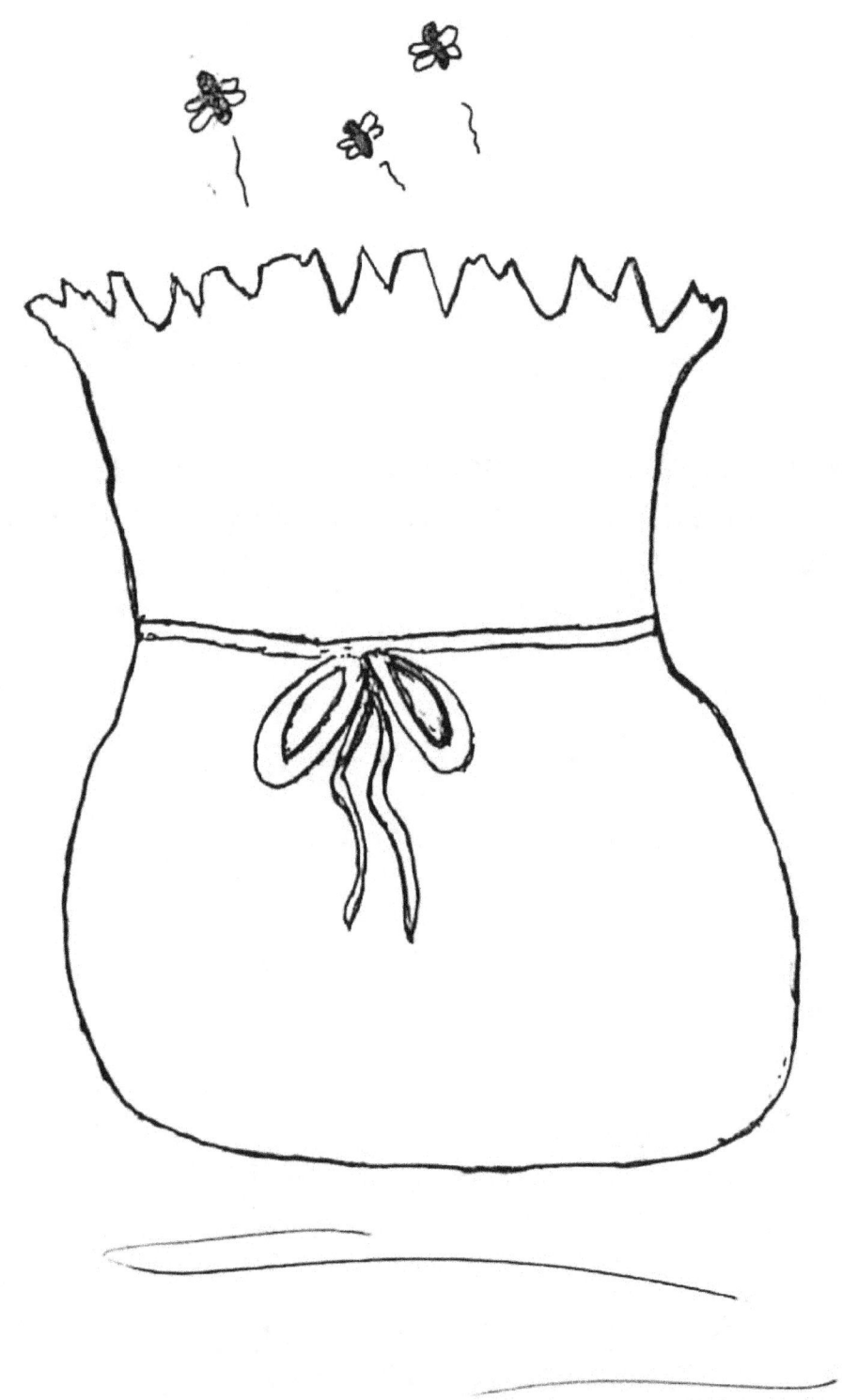

Herbin walked as fast as his little legs could carry him. The sun was just beginning to set as he arrived at the frog pond. He could hear the frogs croaking out their evening songs. Just as he was told to do, he stuck one leg into the water.

Herbin jumped as he heard a very large croak!

The water began to ripple and a large frog floated to the surface. Two big, round, yellow eyes glared at him.

"Who are you and what do you want?" an angry voice asked. Herbin trembled.

"It is I, Mr. Grandfather Frog," Herbin said, his little legs quivering with fear.

"You better have a good reason from waking me up!" Grandfather Frog shouted.

"M-my name is Herbin, and I have a gift for you." Herbin quickly opened the bag of flies the wizard had given him. Instantly, the flies fluttered toward Grandfather Frog who greedily snapped them into his mouth with his quick tongue.

"Mmmmmm," Grandfather frog said once he was done. He was no longer angry. "You must have been sent by Winton the Wizard. How can I help you today, little ant?"

"I was told you could tell me where to get the golden ribbon, so that I can capture the rainbow and take it back to my village, so everyone can believe!"

"Ah, you must be from that little worker ant village. They stopped believing in rainbows a long time ago." Herbin croaked, burping from his full belly of flies.

"You know about my village?" Herbin said, his eyes widening with surprise.

"Little ant, everyone from the village to the forest knows about the worker ants. Their lack of belief is why the rainbow has gone away and will no longer appear to any of us after the rain, " Grandfather frog sadly looked into the sky and continued, " I was but a little tadpole the last time the rainbow graced the sky with her beauty."

"So, there was once a rainbow in my village?"

"Of course! Why, after every rain, the rainbow would appear with her beautiful colors. Everyone would emerge from their shelters after the rainfall, look up into the sky and smile. Oh, the rainbow made everyone so happy." Then, Grandfather Frog's eyes grew dark as he spoke once more.

"It was when those worker ants stopped believing in the rainbow that she went away." he said.

"What happened?"

"It had been two months of no rain and the ants' village was suffering from a terrible drought. The ants grew angry because they had so little food and they began to blame the rainbow for the lack of rain. They shook their little ant fists at the sky and shouted. They decided that they could no longer rely upon the rainbow for their happiness. They turned their backs on the rainbow and forbade anyone in the village from believing in the rainbow ever again. They had to travel miles and miles to get water for their crops from lakes, ponds, and creeks. From that day on, they became known as the worker ants who believed in nothing but work. No rainbows. No dreams. Just work."

"Just hard work!" Herbin repeated with a frown.

"So, it is up to you to make them believe again. Go, get that magical ribbon, find the rainbow, and ask her if she'll let you take her to your village of worker ants, so that they can believe again, and so that she can visit them and bring beauty to the village once more."

"Mr. Grandfather Frog, where might I find the magical ribbon?"

"It is but two-day's travel from here. You must continue on through the forest until you reach a hill covered with the most beautiful flowers you've ever seen. Then you must climb all the way to the top of the hill. Once you reach the top, you have to wait until just before the next sunrise when the sun peaks her golden head above the horizon. You must then ask the sun to give you one of her golden ribbons, so that you can help your village believe in rainbows once again."

"What if the sun doesn't give me one of her golden ribbons?"

"You'll need to take a gift to the sun," said Grandfather Frog, croaking. "Take this bag of sunflower seeds and plant them at the top of the hill." Grandfather Frog handed Herbin a small pouch of seeds. The bag was wet to the touch, and Herbin grimaced at the bag's sogginess.

"Yes, they are wet because seeds need water to grow. Plant these as soon as you get to the top of the hill and they will grow before the sunrise. The sun will see the sunflowers when she peeks her head above the horizon and will be very happy as she loves sunflowers. And so, she will be more likely to help you."

Herbin thanked Grandfather Frog and began his two-day's journey to the hill. He hoped that the sun would be kind and help him with his mission. The forest was dark and scary and, at times, Herbin thought of turning around and abandoning his mission. He had travelled a long distance, and he was very tired, yet he had to help his village believe once again. But first, he had to get that ribbon.

What if the worker ants in his village still didn't believe even after seeing the rainbow? Herbin thought.

Herbin shook the thought right out of his head. He had to believe that his mission would be successful and so, when he finally reached the foot of the hill, he began to climb. Soon his tiny little leg muscles began to ache from climbing. Sweat began to form on his tiny little forehead and his little body began to tremble. Just when he thought that he could not go any further, he reached the top of the hill. Right away, he planted the sunflower seeds. Then he lay down and fell asleep.

He awoke just before sunrise and noticed several strong sunflower plants towering above him, their faces pointed in the direction of the approaching sunrise.

"I am pleased, young ant, with your gift of beauty that you have planted for me to see today," a gentle voice said. Herbin felt his body warm beneath the sun's soft glow. The sun smiled at him.

"Now, what may I do for you before my workday begins, since you have been so kind to me?" The sun asked.

"Madame Sun, I was wondering if you'd be able to spare me one of your golden rays of sunlight so that I might use it to take the rainbow to my village." Madame Sun remained silent as she pondered Herbin's request.

"I don't give my golden ribbons to just anyone, young ant. My ribbons are things of great beauty and must only be used in a manner that shows others great beauty. Tell me why you want to use my golden beauties to take the rainbow from the sky to your village." Madame Sun's face grew brighter with each passing moment.

" I-I, " Herbin stammered. "I want to help my village to believe again." Herbin waited as the sun silently pushed herself above the horizon, a stern look upon her glowing face.

"Ah, you must be from that little worker ant village that stopped believing a long time ago, " Madame Sun said. "Yes, I have heard about them and how they greatly offended our darling Miss Rainbow. I will give you one of my golden ribbons - but only one - so be careful and use it wisely." Madame Sun rose to her full height, her beams of sunlight warming the dew-kissed grass. Before she climbed further into the sky, she plucked a thin golden ribbon from her head and it fell onto the ground in front of Herbin's tiny feet.

Before Madam Sun continued her dawn journey, she gave Herbin instructions as to how to get the rainbow to agree to be led to his village. He would have to help her get there with the golden ribbon.

Herbin thanked Madame Sun and set out upon his journey. It was a long and beautiful way to the land where Miss Rainbow lived. Along his route, he met many nice and friendly creatures who gave him food and shelter when he was tired. Herbin was happy. He would finally be able to help his village!

When Herbin reached the place where Miss Rainbow lived, he did as he was instructed by Madame Sun. He gave Miss Rainbow a pot of liquid sun because she always enjoyed looking at the sun even though the two could never meet. She was overjoyed with Herbin's gift and agreed to go with him so that he could bring happiness and belief to his ant village once again.

At last, Herbin was back at the village but he suddenly became nervous.

Miss Rainbow said to Herbin, "This is where your work ends. Let me do the rest. You have traveled long and far and now it is time that you rest. It is night now in the village and I will appear after the rain in the morning. For now, I will hide behind these trees and, after the last drop of rain falls, you shall see me in the sky. Rest now, my sweet and courageous friend. Tomorrow is going to be a great day!"

Herbin did not sleep well that night. He worried about what the villagers would think of him. He wondered if his father would be angry with him. He wondered if his father would finally believe in rainbows. If no one believed, Herbin's hard work would all have been for nothing.

Eventually, Herbin's eyes grew heavy and he fell asleep on his soft bed. That night, it rained. The rain pounded the ground and splashed mud everywhere throughout the village. Herbin tossed and turned in bed as the rain beat upon the door of his family's little home. His parents were sound asleep. Little did they know what would be awaiting them in the morning.

The next morning, Herbin decided not to go outside. He was afraid. He was so very afraid. Suddenly, he heard sounds he had never heard before. He heard whistling. He heard laughter, and he heard the sounds of little ant children at play.

What Herbin didn't hear was the loud smashing of iron tools from work being done in the middle of the village. He also didn't hear the usual hustle and bustle of worker ants rushing off to their various jobs. He did not hear his father complaining over the morning newspaper as his mother buzzed around the kitchen making breakfast.

Unsure of what to do, Herbin slowly creaked open his bedroom door. He tiptoed down the hallway and noticed that all of his nine thousand nine hundred ninety-nine brothers and sisters were nowhere to be found. He crept into the kitchen but found it empty, too.

Where had everyone gone?

What were these happy sounds, sounds he had only dreamed about hearing?

"Son, come out here," he heard his father yell. *Was he angry?* Had Herbin's efforts upset his father?

Begrudgingly, Herbin slowly made his way to the opened front door where his father stood looking outside.

"Yes, dad?" Herbin gulped.

"Would you just look at all this," Herbin's father said. Herbin remained silent and afraid. Suddenly, his father turned to him and laughed.

"I never thought I'd see her again," said Herbin's father, his eyes filling with tears of joy.

Herbin's own eyes grew wide with amazement as he saw all of his nine thousand nine hundred ninety-nine brothers and sisters playing beneath the rainbow with their worker hats off and their laughter filling the air.

"Isn't she beautiful?" Herbin's father asked, pointing to Miss Rainbow.

"Yes, she is, Dad. Yes, she is." Herbin said, smiling.

"We drove her away, you know, son. We blamed her and she went away, "

"You mean, you're not mad?"

"Of course, not, son! She has given us another chance to believe in her again!" Herbin's father turned to look at his son. "And son, I am asking you to give me another chance to see the world as you do."

Herbin hugged his father tightly.

"I love you, Dad." Herbin said.

"I love you, too, son."

From that day on, the worker ant village was happy. No longer would they spend all their long hours working beneath the sun. They learned how to take breaks and to enjoy the beauty that the rainbow had brought to them after the rain.

About the Author

Dr. Candace Nadine Breen is a West African American who was born and raised in Providence, Rhode Island. She currently lives in Barrington, Rhode Island with her husband, their two children and their two cats.